the Green Mother goose

Saving the World One Rhyme at a Time

by Jan Peck and David Davis

illustrated by Carin Berger

STERLING

New York / London

Contents

The Green Mother Goose

Together we'll do it—
We'll help save the Earth,
Our emerald home,
The place of our birth.
Come now, rhyme with me,
Let's turn our hearts loose,
And fly 'round the world
With Green Mother Goose.

One, Two, We Can Renew

One, two,
We can renew.
Three, four,
We can do more.
Five, six,
Our world to fix.
Seven, eight,
We're not too late.
Nine, ten,
Time to begin!

If All the World Were Stinky

If all the world were stinky,
And our water black as ink,
If toxic rains filled up our drains,
What would we have to drink?

If all the world were stinky,
Our skies fouled without care,
If there were no trees in the summer breeze,
What would we breathe for air?

This Little Piggy

This little piggy saved some water,

This little piggy biked for fun,

This little piggy used windmills,

This little piggy used sun.

And this little piggy squealed,

"Re-re-recycle!"

All the way home.

Yankee Doodle

Yankee Doodle went to town,
A-riding on a trolley,
He made it there in record time,
And rode with sister, Molly.

Yankee Doodle keep it up,
Yankee Doodle Dandy,
Conserve the fuel in your tank,
Keep other options handy.

Yankee Doodle went to school,
A-riding in a carpool,
Sharing rides with all his friends
And using much less car fuel.

Yankee Doodle keep it up,
Yankee Doodle Dandy,
Conserve the fuel in your tank,
Keep other options handy.

Yankee Doodle went to Gran's,
Upon a sturdy gray horse.
Pony saved on gasoline
By eating grass, of course!

Yankee Doodle keep it up,
Yankee Doodle Dandy,
Conserve the fuel in your tank,
Keep other options handy.

Yankee Doodle went to camp,
Upon a shiny, blue bike.
Proud to use his muscle power . . .
Perhaps next time he will hike!

Yankee Doodle keep it up,
Yankee Doodle Dandy,
Conserve the fuel in your tank,
Keep other options handy.

Old Mother Hubbard

Old Mother Hubbard
Went to her cupboard,
To get her poor dog a snack.
She wanted to share,
But junk food was there,
So the poor dog just
rolled on his back.

She went to the store
For food, in a panic,
But when she came home
He wanted organic.

She went to the store
For a beef bone or two,
But when she returned
He begged for tofu.

She went to the market
To buy only local.
Dog bounced and barked.
His approval was vocal.

She markets today
With cloth shopping bags,
And when she gets home
Her dog is all wags!

This Is the Seed That Jack Sowed

This is the seed that Jack sowed.

This is the father who mulched the mound.

He hugged the mother who gardened the ground.

She kissed the daughter with pigtails unwound,

Who gathered the eggs shaped oval and round,

That were laid by the hen all feathered and fat,

That gobbled the berries fit for the kings,

That grew for the bee with the buzzing wings,

That kissed the blooms,

That basked in the sun,

That beamed on the bush,

That soaked up the rain,

That watered the soil,

That covered the seed that Jack sowed.

Mary, Mary, Quite Contrary

Mary, Mary, quite contrary,
Refused to garden green.
Her toxic sprays, a choking haze,
Spreading dangers, hurtful and mean.

Organic Mary, not contrary,
How does your garden grow?
With ladybug smiles and compost piles,
And pretty herbs all in a row.

Little Boy Green

"Little Boy Green,
Come blow your horn,
Plant trees in the forest,
Make fuel from the corn.
And where is the boy
Who prunes all the trees?"

"He's out by the beehive,
Tending the bees."

Little Jack Horner

Little Jack Horner
Changed bulbs in the corner,
Replacing the old incandescents.
Now the lamps on the sills
Cut his mama's high bills,
'Cause the lights are
all compact fluorescents.

Jack Sprat

Jack Sprat ate fast-food fat,
His wife ate leafy greens.
Now she is fit, and healthy, too,
While Jack's outgrown his jeans!

There Was a Little Girl
Who Had a Little Curl

There was a little girl who had a little curl—
On top of her head it glittered.
When she was good, she recycled all she could,
But when she was bad—

SHE
LITTERED.

Recycle
Man

Recycle, recycle,
Recycle man,
Sort all the trash
As fast as you can.

Take it, remake it,
And mark it with a **P**,
And reuse it all later,
For the Planet and me!

Here We Go Round the Neighborhood

Here we go round the neighborhood,
The neighborhood, the neighborhood.
Here we go round the neighborhood
One bright and sunny morning.

This is the way we pick up the trash,
Pick up the trash, pick up the trash.
This is the way we pick up the trash
One bright and sunny morning.

This is the way we recycle our cans,
Recycle our cans, recycle our cans.
This is the way we recycle our cans
One bright and sunny morning.

This is the way we plant our trees,
Plant our trees, plant our trees.
This is the way we plant our trees
One bright and sunny morning.

This is the way we tend our park,
Tend our park, tend our park.
This is the way we tend our park
One bright and sunny morning.

If All the Seas Were One Sea

If all the seas were one sea,

What a great sea that would be.

If all the trees were one tree,

What a great tree that would be.

If all the men were one man,

What a great man he would be.

And if the great man cared greatly

For the tree, the sea, and me,

What a great world this would be!

Sister Moon and Brother Sun

Sister Moon and Brother Sun,

Bless our world when day is done.

Four gentle prayers for Mother Earth,

Four angels round her head:

One for sun and one for rain

And two to heal the Earth again.

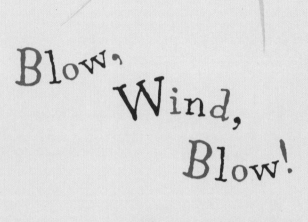

Blow, Wind, Blow!

Blow, wind, blow!

Turn, windmill, fast!

Make clean power that can last,

And send it here for a kid like me,

And light my lamp so I can see.

Blow, wind, blow!

Shine, sun, shine!

Sunbeam rays!

Make clean power all my days,

And send it here for a kid like me,

Clean and warm and bright and free.

Shine, sun, shine!

Mary Had a Little Lamb

Mary had a little lamb,
Its fleece was snowy white,
But they lived near a coal-fired plant—
Now its fleece is black as night.

Mary and her little lamb
Now work for cleaner air:
Seeking ways to spread the word
To make their friends aware.

Old King Coal

Old King Coal was a powerful soul,

A powerful soul was he.

He made lots of money,

And he thought life was sunny,

When he called for his limousines three.

Now Old King Coal is a better old soul,

A better old soul is he.

Though he was a meanie,

Now he is a greenie,

And he works to keep our skies smoke-free.

Jack Be Nimble

Jack be nimble,
Jack be fun—
Turn off the tap,
Don't let it run.

Jack be nimble,
Jack be slick—
Please close the door
And come in quick.

Jack be nimble,
Jack be bright—
Leaving a room,
Switch off the light.

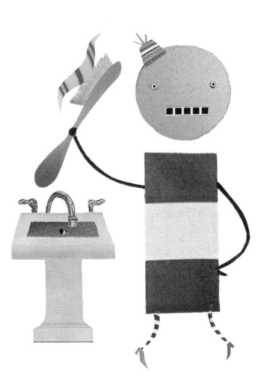

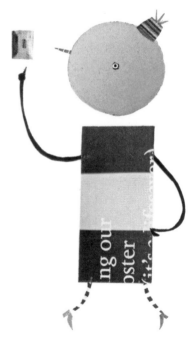

Jack be nimble,
Jack be sweet—
Please use both sides
Of every sheet.

Jack be nimble,
Jack be fine—
Dry your wet clothes
Out on the line.

Jack is nimble,
Jack is smart.
He's a helper.
He did his part!

Humpty Dumpty

Humpty Dumpty sat on the fence.

Humpty Dumpty couldn't make sense—

Was the world warming? He wouldn't decide.

Now Humpty Dumpty is totally fried!

Humpty Dumpty now understands.

Humpty Dumpty is lending his hands.

Now he is wiser, and perched in a cup.

Professor Dumpty is sunny-side up!

Little King Pippin

Little King Pippin built a straw-baled hall

And mixed up adobe to plaster the wall.

With double-paned windows and southern exposure

The fine home he planned had a courtyard enclosure.

The greenest of kings—and his home was the proof.

He put solar panels on top of his roof.

King Pippin lived happily all of his days,

His house shaded by trees and warmed by sun rays.

Three Wise Mice

Three wise mice,
Three wise mice,
See how they save!
See how they save!

They search for clothes at the thrift store shops,
Recycle the treasures at yard sale stops,
Catch water from rain and use all the drops.
Three wise mice!

Hickety, Pickety, Free-Range Hen

Hickety, Pickety, free-range hen,
Speckle-feathered clucking friend.
Hen is thrilled 'cause she's cage-free,
She'll lay great eggs for you and me.
Sometimes nine, and sometimes ten,
Hickety, Pickety, free-range hen.

Jack and Jill

Jack and Jill went up the hill
To fetch a pail of water.
At the top, they saved each drop,
And filled the day with laughter.

Jack and Jill ran down the hill
And brought their pail of water.
They sowed seeds and pulled some weeds,
Happily ever after.

Hickory, Dickory, Dock

Hickory, dickory, dock,
Our world is on the clock.
We must learn how
To love Earth now!
Hickory, dickory, dock.

Rub-a-Dub-Dub

Rub-a-dub-dub—
Babes covered in mud!
They need a bath before night.
But the water flow's slow
And the soap's running low.
How can they set things a-right?

Rub-a-dub-dub—
Three babes in one tub,
Each splashing 'round like an otter.
One sang, "I'm no dunce,
If we scrub all at once,
We'll save lots of soap
And hot water!"

I Saw a Ship A-Sailing

I saw a ship a-sailing,
A-sailing on the sea,
A-hauling frozen green fruit
'Round half the world to me.

I saw a local farmer
Sell produce on the pier.
It took no oil to bring it,
Because he grew it here.

I saw just what was needed,
It didn't take me long.
I bought fruit from the farmer . . .
He sang a happy song.

There Was an Old Woman Who Lived in a Shoe

There was an old woman
Who lived in a shoe.
Though the place was too drafty,
Her kids knew *just* what to do.

They sealed up the laces,
Insulated the toe.
They bought compact fluorescents
To save her some dough.

They built solar panels,
Windmills in the field.
After all of their hard work,
You'd say she's well-heeled!

This Is Our Garden Earth

This is our garden Earth:

In that garden there is a country,

In that country there is a city,

In that city there is a neighborhood,

In that neighborhood there is a street,

On that street there stands a house,

In that house there is a room,

In that room there is a child,

And in that child there is a dream . . .

A dream to save our garden Earth.

Dream in the child,

Child in the room,

Room in the house,

House on the street,

Street in the neighborhood,

Neighborhood in the city,

City in the country,

Country in the garden:

This is our garden Earth.

To my mother, Phyllis Gail McComb (1920-2008), who taught me to love
and respect nature, and allowed me to raise all kinds of orphaned animals:
blue jays, baby possums, ring-neck doves, a red-eared turtle named Frisky,
a crow, a squirrel, and a mole, as well as many cats and dogs.
—J.P.

To my "Grandpaw," Raymond Lacy (1905-1997), a farmer, fisherman,
outdoorsman, and unbribed soul.
— D.D.

To Mom, with love and gratitude.
— C.B.

STERLING and the distinctive Sterling logo are registered trademarks of
Sterling Publishing Co., Inc.

Library of Congress Cataloging-in-Publication Data

Peck, Jan.
The green Mother Goose : saving the world one rhyme at a time / by Jan
Peck and David Davis ; illustrated by Carin Berger.
p. cm.
ISBN 978-1-4027-6525-4
1. Children's poetry, American. 2. Nursery rhymes, American. I.
Davis, David, 1948 Oct. 29- II. Berger, Carin, ill. III. Title.
PS3566.E246G74 2011
811'.54--dc22
2010030638
Lot#:
2 4 6 8 10 9 7 5 3 1
1/11
Published by Sterling Publishing Co., Inc.
387 Park Avenue South, New York, NY 10016
Text © 2011 by Jan Peck and David Davis
Illustrations © 2011 by Carin Berger
Distributed in Canada by Sterling Publishing
c/o Canadian Manda Group, 165 Dufferin Street
Toronto, Ontario, Canada M6K 3H6
Distributed in the United Kingdom by GMC Distribution Services
Castle Place, 166 High Street, Lewes, East Sussex, England BN7 1XU
Distributed in Australia by Capricorn Link (Australia) Pty. Ltd.
P.O. Box 704, Windsor, NSW 2756, Australia

Printed in China
All rights reserved.

Sterling ISBN 978-1-4027-6525-4

For information about custom editions, special sales, premium and
corporate purchases, please contact Sterling Special Sales
Department at 800-805-5489 or specialsales@sterlingpublishing.com.

Designed by Mina Chung
The illustrations were created using collage with found papers and ephemera.

This book is printed with soy-based inks on paper from mixed sources:
well-managed forests, controlled sources, and recycled wood or fiber.
Certified by the Forest Stewardship Council.